THE RAIN CHILDREN

— Stride —

THE RAIN CHILDREN

David H.W. Grubb

for Beverly

THE RAIN CHILDREN
First edition 1993
© David Grubb
All rights reserved

ISBN 1 873012 54 3 *(paperback)*
ISBN 1 873012 55 1 *(hardback)*

Cover art © Bruce Bitmead 1993

Acknowledgements
*Ambit, Ex-Calibre, Symphony, The 3rd Half, Contemporary Review,
Rialto, Spokes, Spoils* (The Poetry Business Anthology 90/91),
Neon Lilly Tiger (Maypole Editions Anthology 1993),
Staple, Arcadian, The Green Book, Stride.

Published by
STRIDE
37 Portland Street
Exeter
Devon
EX1 2EG
England

Contents

QUESTIONS TO MY PARENTS

THE VIEW FROM THE TREEHOUSE

The view from the treehouse
is the view within. Boys certain
of escape, escapade, release. To climb
above ordinary events, to tower here,
to celebrate bedlam and disdain.

Grounded adults, hedged in things of
the linear universe, tied down and flat.
But up here, in a house with no rooms,
we are shipwreck and island, Gulliver
and Gestapo, a watchtower and space machine.

In autumn mist, slippery as secrets,
we spy on the cemetery. In summer
we litter the deck with comics
and prepare to repel a gang of girls.

In a ruin of rain our skull and crossbones
nearly collides with the nearest foe,
or we head for Berlin, the stench of grease
and metal vile, the wind shrieking
with flails of barbed wire.

And once the view from the treehouse
was of Maureen who had come to work for us
and had somewhere got a baby. She stood beneath
our tree quite unaware of its spies
and punched a man in the face before embracing him.

The view from the treehouse must still be there
although the nails and planks and ropes have gone.
And the house has been demolished and there are
nice little dwellings and all the trees have been cut down;
but the view, the view itself must still be there.

IN SHINING NIGHT

In these gardens, these declarations, these codes
I see my mother carefully collecting the large lilies,
sacred flowers, fragments of dance, the huge stamen
like an improbable tongue within the ghost demise; the measure
always of silence, of peace, of coiled respect, of naiveté.
And my father fumbling his favourite fictions still, the fag
sticking to his lips to seize the stammer, to halt despair,
always denying his doubt, always forging new adventures, fresh
etiquette; the bells of reason so ordinary, so cheap, so cold.
And now, you're gone, run out, surpassed, I admire what I despised,
I made famous and fabulous. The order re-ordered. The anger collapsed
into a stained glass window. I see the boy in the vicarage garden
with his uncertain smile, his stooped dreams, his secret pledge. And it is
always the large houses that collect, beckon, token;
the ancient trees and autumn lawns and rejected beacons of church bells.
The terror of reality. The hunched shadows of truth. The clamour
of doubt. The rooms in huge houses crowded with adults content
to cry. The old bandaging their ruins in cadenzas of creed.
The caw caw of the rooks reeling in circles of jeopardy,
the progress of dreams stretching in the clouds of dawn,
the wild grass of Cornish cliffs turning on wheat white tides.
In shining night the carol of stars.

BENEATH CEDAR BOUGHS

Beneath this tree grandfather sat to consider
what words might mean in his sermon. And
when mother was very ill the doctor made her
rest here whilst she gathered strength for
the operation. And here we stared at the sun
from the swing, the old chain creaking, the
sky jigsawed by cedar boughs, the bark
like ancient skins, the smell of dark oil
and old garments, always suggesting heat,
an energy locked in, stored, old as stone.
And here we picked up the dead hedgehog
(once we were brave enough), and carried it in
a towel to place it on the sundial as if
somehow something might touch it, give
back the silent life, the mystery of its song.
And we sat, chins on knees, the smell
of cedar descending, descending, the late
afternoon light escaping, the dampness
growing, the two wood pigeons making
ready, claiming territory, the swing
waiting like a curious thing for some
young acrobat, to swing so high,
to be held in space, between evening and
night, between the deaths of small
animals and the secrets of their lives.

DISPOSING OF THE CEDAR

Now they have come to dispose of the cedar tree.
First we took down the rusting swing, then father
arrived with his camera for once not asking us to pose,
content with an image of village men and six children
and mother calling the dogs into the house to safety.
After two hours of fixing ropes and axing and sawing
in the right places she is ready to fall, somehow
not quite ready to let go for ever and let in the light
where all of my childhood there have been waves
of green, of sweeping peaceful islands, of deep and
graceful wings of green. And now, now, slowly
at first, the terrible crunching as if glass were
being rammed, as if metal were being screwed in a knot,
as if a boulder were crunching chickens to pulp,
this vast island falls across the lawn, across the light,
across what we have seen for years, across our childhood,
across the huge expectancy of these seconds. And now
the men stand there, quite still, considering the power
of the cedar tree, the locked-in energy, its creation,
and we watch them and observe their awkwardness and
wait for the youngest man to begin his swearing.

ANOTHER ENERGY

What would you have us do now? Gather in
all the achievements of faith and come to your funeral
with nothing but conviction, my sister so distressed,
my wife and daughters catching hold of your summer days
when afternoon tea was a feast and you waved us farewell
across the ragged rose beds, the garden warning us?
Friends came from Somerset and after the service we
recalled your energy, your loyalty, your determination
to smile and always find the light. And now, four months
later, we are ready to bury the ashes, the small urn,
in Cornwall where all the childhood memories began.
Will it be a sea wind wail again, the gulls bobbing
like lost kites, or the blue grey sea music, the
rooks rocking the tall trees, the same ancient land
and earth struggling to recreate, stone walls packed deep
in another energy? And what would you have us do now,
preparing for this final ceremony, this necessary
departure, this saying farewell again,
when you've been so much with us, even closer now,
simply changing your meaning to our lives?

TWO WEEKS AFTER MY FATHER'S DEATH WE PICK THE PEARS

Two weeks after my father's death we pick the pears from five trees.
My mother wanted to leave them but here I am swinging in this tree.
The pears are ready. We have timed it just right.
Old bark bruises my back; green dust gets into my sweat.
I work until the moon starts its first rattle across the sea.

Each pear is handed down and inspected by mother.
Kneeling on the steps she places each fruit in a box.
Every pear has to be looked at carefully. There is order
here and some craft.

This is no time to be afraid. In the coming months
I can see her treating letters, papers, words, memory
in the same way.

MOTHER, STOOPING IN THE EARLY LIGHT

For Sara

Mother, stooping in the early light,
inspecting the lilies, their cold flames, their silences.
She adjusts the complicated heating mechanism and the oil heaters
in the immense conservatory with tiled floor and wrought iron
decorations. She is an expert at this. Each year she is
bringing them on or holding them back to be ready
for Easter morning. From this protected territory they
will be gently carried in baskets and slowly driven to
the neighbouring churches. Each one has kept a week
of holy silence, the dark shades of contemplation
holding a dense glow. But she must be ahead
of all this, making ready for these flags of success,
their glow held in a single flame of adoration,
to remind us of a survival, the resurrection trick,
the flowers in the early light now responding
to her skills, her respect; each one like a
novice; a young woman preparing for a dance;
a bloom that will radiate what our words
cannot quite express. And my mother stands
there now, her delivery list carefully confirmed,
each lily fragile as ancient glass, waiting
for the light to rise and rise, unfurling the
fertility of faith.

GOING OUT

Mother, going out with her carols, her small tones,
her song that took over the words, consumed all meaning;
finally her hands quite still, each finger finishing its energy,
so that in my arms I held a head simply, the soft soft
going out, releasing this meaning;
and we were left with essential, practical details;
prayers and songs and some other person's words of comfort.

STILLED

What would I say to my father
the years pulling him away;
but his mind, ah his mind
sits at the table like a giant visitor.

We dress the mind in old images
but it wants to talk to the children.
We spread stories over it
and it describes white horses.

On Sunday the mind is louder
than church bells, lither than
butterflies; creaking and crackling
it blows its bubbles.

We throw it some prayers, a
joke or two; or we attempt ignorance,
talking very loudly about how things
have improved, the glorious new.

The only place where it is stilled
is in the small garden; all day it
plays within the wind, the night
stars gather it up like a baby.

ALONE

She would like there to be someone
there to share the start of this day.
Her single spoon and knife settle by
the bowl, the cup and saucer, the side
plate, the napkin ring she insists upon.
And she will sit here, alone, the day
commencing, the morning ready to go,
the gulls in the bay screwing sounds
from the other side, the other reality.
She sits, consumes, sticks to this
ritual, this essential trick of
conformity. The beginning to each
day smells of tea and toast and on
Sundays a hard boiled egg. And
ever the second chair, always there,
at the side of her, as if some day
there will be a guest, a visitor. She
has it placed there, always there.
She would like to share the start
of this day. She would like to speak
of it to somebody other than the radio
person, the newspaper voice, the whisper
of her dress and other things. She sees
sometimes how the bones of her fingers
and the handle of the knife have grown
alike. Ivory. Paled with age. Once
beautiful. She would like there to be
someone there, to be there, to be here.

ALWAYS BURYING MY FATHER

Always burying my father, who will not lie down,
the words clinging to the bone of dream, the short fictions of hope;
who is it who enters the door each day, smiles and frowns,
the festivity of remembering, the essential soliliquies of no?

It is easier to greet him now, distance reduces us all,
and even his eccentric dress can be a pleasure; the boom becomes
a song and where we stumbled is saved by a joke, a call
to retreat, an agreement to disagree at hates and loves.

And now it is too late to tell him I forgive, seated
at his desk, his pipe rack neatly placed between the books,
one drawer still locked, the key lost, as if small secrets
were waiting there; an image of winter in his summer truths.

GHOSTS

I am waiting for my father's ghost
to arrive across the crowded room and shout
I am sorry. I love you.

I am waiting for his ghost to put down the terrible
cigarette butt, the Bible bulging with silences, and say
I agree. I am sorry. I am with you.

I am waiting in the field of sea music, the forest of rags,
the glade of drums, for his ghost to arrive in Wagnerian
propensities, to leap from the light that belches from crevices
to proclaim peace, acceptance, arrival, No Smoking.

Meanwhile words still gather in huge rooms, mirrors dance
gently together; I grow older and the wisdom slips down
between library silences, images of cold stone, windows
looking out onto abandoned tennis courts.

THE TERROR OF THE LAST QUOTATIONS

The old men fearing what their wives might say
took to their gardens, their sheds and garages and their boys
to tree houses.

From the tree houses the boys looked out at gardens
piled high with words, anecdotes, bad jokes and
stale dreams.

In the sheds where spiders ticked, the men could
smell the old straw, sacking, stiff newspapers,
and in the garages the grease creaked,
gently shifted.

What the old men dreaded, feared most
was about to happen, beyond the logic of stacked dishes,
the cool order of flower vases, the efficacy of peas.

Perhaps it would come from dark hat boxes,
old lace, the biscuit tin waiting to begin,
the centre of the ball of wool.

QUESTIONS TO MY PARENTS

In this garden, then, they appear,
with the grey green of cedar boughs
and the well mown lawn and just in
view the deck chairs and my grandparents'
summerhouse. Is it summer or early
autumn and are there doves in the tree?
Is it real or dream and are those smiles
for me or all that they can remember between?
Is it a poem or a prayer or the
planet we have become?

A SMALL SOLACE

After her burial, the soft blooms of their words,
he stands in the garden, the real day broken away.

Their coming here, their travel was kindness,
but now he needs space, totality, silences.

Not that there can be speech, signs, a ghost;
the dark kitchen warned him of this.

But a place that cannot be crowded, a small
solace of territory, the green leaf warm.

And only now can he raise up his face
and let the light trace his tears.

A NUMBERS GAME

One was my grandfather gripped by religion telling truth.
Two the hunt for freedom in the flags of the ancient dead.
Three the trees cascading with stars.

And then it ends. I do not know where to go. I freeze in
my solace. I hear the sacraments of texts. I let go
the planet and plunge into sleep.

THE BLUE CHAIR

For Clare & Emily

I

The fiction of fact and one's deliverance from it
so that from the blue chair one is able to come across
recollections and recognitions and still see the distance
as new, discovery, fable, acceptable. And always the
comfort of voices, stories, anecdotes, the poetry of reconciliation;
the postcard of one's life perched in an obvious place as if we were
about to let loose in mad balloons, sail above certainty, or
build wings of disdain; or having written thin postscripts we
close the door, take a black and white train, a sepia journey
to the ice lands, the distant cold, to let the fear freeze
on the page in the ice-capped mind. The need for such escapes
as one seeks deliverance. The need of knowledge when all the time
the diary declares who we really are, the letter posted in our mind
screams betrayal, the song cannot be sung, the dance would
break our legs. And so it is this thing, this huge thought,
that catches us yet again between the sea path that calls
and the dream we cannot totally recall and still the dictation of
desires. The ordinary door. The simple window glass. The blue
chair in the sun or in the rain. A sudden image of boys
racing into the centre of the field in the midst of a thunderstorm;
braced into bravery, hurling caution, demanding courage.
In the centre of the field willing each one of us to stand still
and stare at the evening green sky, the tall terror of it,
the hurtling rags of it, the brawling beasts of it,
the ripped skins of drums and warrior flags and bandit rage,
the tribal ruin of it; waiting for it to fall, to fall,
to discover us there, to consume our status and souls.

II

And it is this ordinary door that opens to other rooms
where our lives collide or collect in hallways of memory as the sea
gently washes against the grandfather clock, the waves lap a
green tea trolley, my grandmother falls out of her heaped bed

and tennis rackets float out of the bay like biscuit-thin banjos.
And I see my mother again in the rose garden, her white hair filled
with moths, her mind muddled in a psalm of petals and apple
blossoms and calm orchards of Somerset. My father again chasing
the Chinese geese into the small barn, his mind dazzled with
carols and Irish ancestors, the church clock striking bats
and doves, gulls strutting on his typewriter in the study
strewn with family charts, Quaker diaries, the creak of country
houses, sermons scratching their solemnities across his dreams.
And lost in a tree house, in an air balloon, in a space rocket,
in a stage coach, racing between cedar boughs and the
scream of vultures, I meet again the boy hiding from Latin
declensions, the tricks of arithmetic, the appaling thuggery
of physics, the declarations of blank pages. And the drive
to the vicarage again fills with faces of the dead. And
the small bedroom cupboard heaves with beasts. And the
curtains if they were to be drawn back would reveal the
curses of Custer and Captain Ahab and the eagle eyes
of Geronimo, the bowed down compulsion of Captain Scott.
Snow climbs onto the bed end. Sea runs beneath
the door. Ice enters the tuck box.

III

Sitting again in the blue chair, the garden slipping into evening
and the tulip fires now cooling, one is again aware of the blackbird's
warning signal. Is it the cat prowling along the garden wall or the
woman next door banging away at the telephone or perhaps the green
umbrella gently flaying as if it has just remembered the thrill of
flight? And we are lifted up, rise above this gentle scene, the
commuters racing to the car park and the secretaries with clicking heels
not seeing us as we float above the roof tops now heading for
the hills. The blackbird falls silent. The houses disappear. Even
the church tower and the tallest trees vanish as we enter a cloud
of sublime silence. The green umbrella and the garden table and chairs
have risen with us. The wine glasses and the Sunday newspapers
and my wife's sunglasses remain fixed to the table and the cloud
carries us higher until the light filters to stars and a nearby
aircraft passes us like a silver pencil, totally silent. And

the blue chair itself has become silver in this flight.
Its sturdy frame assures me that this is not a dream. The
cloud departs and we are left in the arc of a mystery. The
trick is never to question, to sip some more wine, to ignore
the newspaper which belongs to another reality, the umbrella
also. We can remain here for hours. We can count
the stars and wait for the sun to come up from somewhere.
We can accept all this, believing all the time in the
certainty of the silver light and the sound of the wings
that are always near, gently moving with us, gently
growing larger and larger until all we can sense is this
power of flight, this space to travel, this precision.

PRIEST

PRIEST

I.

And when each one of them had left
after the convivial shuffling of pleasantries,
only a few with any words of real meaning
and those who could never look him in the mind,
he always remained in the church awhile,
silent within the heaped prayers as if they
also waited before entering the coil of their commission,
perhaps filtering between the fears and ambitions and
what was fact rather than loose frames of fiction.
It was as if the seconds between the ending of some
major work of music and the massive din of applause
were delayed, as if something else were to come,
as if the God would not so easily accept this
incantation of desires, the ritual and respect
had to fall away to reveal what meaning meant.

II.

And at times this was indeed the only time
that he could enter the silence that he longed for,
when nothing was expected of him, when his own words
could pitch behind what others made of them, the
haul of duty and liturgy, each prayer and text loaded
with expectation, coils of custom and convention, so
that each second was plundered by necessity, what could
be easily identitified and consumed smothering the pause
to doubt, to wrench out a new meaning, to compel
the soul onwards as if there were only this radiant path.
Then this silence, this great escape, as if he had the power
to dismantle it all, to dismiss every bit of it, to
stand up now and say this was no more than passionate
muttering, not the belief but the confusion of faith,
not the statement but the dream of its need.

III.

It was mostly the seasons that called them back,
even the saddest squires at Christmas, and at Easter
farmers who had given up their fear of God yet haunted
by the bark of bells, the green man skipping into their dreams,
the tall ghosts of elemental trysts. And when they were not
here to name or claim they lifted their dead with flowers,
the young men trussed into borrowed suits, the women watching
their children disappear, and a few chewing anger beneath
the bitter text of time, the determination welling in their
minds to hate this God, to dig this land until its blood
were oil or gold, to hack back meaning and carve identity
out from the filth of barns, the reek of sheds, the cold
call of the February field. Some of these men would only
return here once. Some closed doors on reason. A few
heard words like tigers, strode out with flames in their minds.

IV.

Sometimes he lacked what simple exchange was necessary. It was
easier to listen to the women or children. There was a
shadow in the minds of the younger men, some trick of discipline
or disorder so that it was necessary to stick to the
comfortable, the well-observed; they dreaded the stench of
mystery. Or was it history; did they see him coming out of
the village school, a threat to their freedom; was he
woven into the awkwardness of sterile sermons, the rasp of
orthodoxy, the dreaded cant of grey memorials and ornate
guilt cursed at by their fathers, ridiculed in the pub?
The lisp of eccentricity lingered in this rejection. The men
who pulled bells never stayed for the service. It was only
the older men, their huge hands gripping the
hymnal as if it might fly, their awkward singing,
waiting for a single truth, to bury it, to deep enfold.

V.

In the silence of his room the words he would
say waited to become. His sermon always began
from the silence ready to be filled, the open notebook,
the discipline shaping his articulation; the words that
should have come from the meaning now coming as always
to meet him half way, to make a meaning, to give him
the voice that would seldom determine anything but self.
And cast upon the congregation, each mind capable of
self-definition, each life ready to re-order whatever he
said, the words and sentences and flourishes like some small food
that could be partaken quietly, each noise gently setting
down, each hymn slowly consumed, the heads and faces of
people he knew like strangers; no eyes to wink back trust,
no codes to urge him on. It would always be the same.
From the pews their own senses singing back a small song.

VI.

Sometimes seeing the men come home from the fields,
farms, the heat of summer and the stubborn state of winter,
he wished for words that would seal some respect, of
recognition or encounter or defeat. It was not pride.
It was not the sting of satisfaction. It was cold and hard.
Observing Sam Frost at hedge laying he was again aware
of this. Each sapling cut down but not severed, saved to
fuse sap, to give out energy, the bill-hook perfectly shaped
to slice and stop, and finally lacing of another wood along
the top, the tap tap of his sideways axe, the security
of this craft handed on for generations; against wind and the
hurling rain and the defeat of reasons; against storm and doubt
and the self respect abandoned by machines and technology;
against the laws of progression and the fiscal logic and
the giving up of everything stained with blood and expertise.

VII.

He gave them words and he gave the dead man grace.
As usual the dead man was traced by anecdotes; his hobbies,
the hours in his garden, even his jokes; seldom a diary or a
letter; never a curse; and the secrets that may have been
between them were left in the litter of grief, of loss.
And with each comfort he gave them a chance to touch
things they had deserted for years, or had never known,
or had even made fun of. The church, the service, the grace,
or the cremation that seemed tidier if no easier in
the chaotic rocking of their minds. A place to make the
parting real, a ceremony of other people's words, the texts
to beat down the jungle of wrath. The essential considerations
and regulations. He gave them stories and songs to touch,
and held the candles of faith for them and in case they did
not dare light them held out an ancient flame.

VIII.

He stood again in the field of winter feeling the cold,
letting it lift him and wrap him and enter his doubt. It was
real, actual, something to be challenged, and yet welcome.
It told him of his foolishness, his idiotic penitence with
words and songs, the small successes that would all burn down,
finally be lost, inconsequential as each mind closed down to ice.
The doubt was strong as diamond, real in his stomach and soul;
and he wished to describe it in detail, totally recognise its
shape and power in this field of winter, this cold territory
of white sun and broken walls and ugly rusted abandonment.
He caught this doubt in his hands and lifted it up to
the great trees and the white sun and the pitching wind
and held it as high as he could; for the God and angels to
see, its stern attempt at power, its perfect pity.

IX.

Between candle silence burning back on brass
and the light of stained glass clinging to 'amens',
this old confusion of meaning and its fictions, the need
to clarify and yet obedient to the context of mystery.
As if an idol were more certain than a dream, as if
the ending to each prayer were but prelude, as if belief
roared like a huge beast above the small creature of living.
Within the wine the essential concept of betrayal. Within
the bread the slightest fragrance of forgetting. Within the
hymn the roar of sands in the desert places. And the wolf
roams beside the water where we would refresh ourselves, the lizard
creeps over the breasts of the naked women, the place
where a miracle has not yet taken its shape is visited
by wild dogs and bats. Between candles the whispers
of the words of the prayers you have not yet said.

X.

And when each of them has assembled, ready now
for the roar of hallelujahs, the flames of lilies, the
bells to call them out of winter, the figures in the
Easter Garden to let them play again; when they are all
standing beneath this huge power to be above the
day to day, the light so immense now we are immersed
in praise, when all the palms have become trumpets,
what can he do then with his field of winter, his
pack of doubts, his vision of the blind man waiting to
see? He stands in the pulpit with his vocabulary of
charms, the games of prophets and seers in his bag,
the jack in the box's Christ swaying on its spring,
and he hears his own voice and his father's voice and the
voice of the dead farmer and the voice of the youngest
child hurling down the silence, defeating it, excelling.

STANLEY SPENCER
ARRIVING IN HEAVEN

STANLEY SPENCER ARRIVING IN HEAVEN

For Nick and Mary Parry

1.

He is wondering if there might be trees;
and now he sees boughs
crooked and green greeting him.

He is wondering if there might be women;
and now he sees their arms, onion sheen
as they spread the celebration tables.

He is wondering if there might be words;
and now he hears angels gossiping.

2.

It is silent. He opens his mind to a meadow of silence.
The light that falls on everything is the silver of springs,
the brown of deep held rocks, gold of fish kingdoms,
and the heron standing on the far bank
stares out at the splendour which
falls and falls until
the Lord of glory arrives
on His bicycle.

3.

And the light that is falling
is held in the man's mind
as he deciphers his realities,
is deep set in the valley as the sun sets,
is driven in views of the village from a distance,
is present in the hurrying woman who again
makes her way to the chapel with a basket of lilies,
is held in the face of the infant in a large green pram.

4.

Entering Heaven is to leap into such light
that Stanley Spencer has one face at two angles,
has one mind in green and one of snake silver, listens
to saints on one level and a small orchestra on another,
and then there is to be comprehended the saint
picking up his yellow umbrella in a field with a lion.

5.

Spencer attends the roll call.
Spencer is asked to undress.
Spencer has his eyes looked at.
Spencer is asked to explain 'light'.
Spencer is given a chance to sing.
Spencer is left in an orchard of blossom
and told that he must wait.

6.

At a distance so near it comes and goes
in the presence of the dark shrubs which are
all the time changing to gold.
Spencer watches what must be an angel
skinny dipping in what must be a lake.
At a nearness the dark gold body of the
angel who has taken off its wings to
protect an image of perfection. So near
coming and going the dark gold of the angel
who constantly dips beneath the water level
yet is never out of sight the deep water
somehow in sky or part of the air or part
of the body at a distance changing yet.

7.

At intervals with himself Stanley Spencer
begins to dress himself in the clothes that
were left on the large blue table, the blue
having attracted him from the very first moment.
The blue it appeared had got into the clothes
so that the shirt and pullover and tie now hold the
blue. Even the wings he now struggled with
were part of this blue more than the white
he had expected, anticipated, accepted.
Now it was the blue, gradually the blue,
entirely the blue, all being the blue.

8.

Assembled within the light lifting
ideas of the new. His mind not quite departed
and expecting to hold happy conversations with John Donne.
There are no steps to be scrubbed here and there is no difficulty
about departure. The light lifts ideas of the new and an
angel with a Gladstone bag may exceed Stanley's own steep
paradoxes. Ah; such parades, such poetry, such co-ordination.
He wonders now if this is Heaven. He wonders what will follow.
Stanley Spencer is not quite sure of this certainty, the angel with
the Gladstone bag; is he God or John Donne or Christ? Beneath
a bough of apples, Stanley seeks the real sky, the glorious
declaration beyond proof, the tight textures of certainties.
The way he might have come. The entrance he might have made.
The light lifting the scene, everything ascending; his total
awareness rising so that now all images integrate, abandon.
The sense of sense going. The self squeezed away. The light
absorbing his soul. The arching of it, the taking of it, the entire
exultation of light lifting Stanley Spencer into convictions.

THE HURT TERRITORIES

THE HURT TERRITORIES

I.

Always moving away
    from an imagined image.

Who gave it to us, adorned the idea,
    or did we do it ourselves,

the hunter created by the hunter,
    the essential grace of pain?

Always moving between these forces
    so that the yes and no cross or scatter

round us, creep into ruin, split in
    sad attitudes, our father's faces lurking

in the certainty of disorder, the ruins of
    trust, the small gardens of deceit.

And how then do we trust them,
    these ancient men whose strength is death,

or the quiet mothers whose rage stained
    far stronger than any leaping tirade?

Burying our parents in small corners of life,
    the certainty of their failures distilling,

the inherited materials creating their own
    music and mutters and ghosted retreats,

the sad percussion of messages and changed
    meanings and the circus of things not meant.

Leave all things familiar the dreams say,
    each word slipping like a useless glove,

the half told fictions, the folded wisdoms,
a recalled song caught in evening light.

You will not do, you cannot say, but
we always hear you clinging to our silences.

The shape of this planet accesible in a
child's drawing, a reality screwed inside a joke,

the ship in the bottle teasing us like the
photograph album in the junk shop.

Who do we love when we lie down to die
and who stands up for us when we have gone?

A letter in the mad lady's suitcase, a rose
crushed into the fragile family Bible.

A fable we have rehearsed all of our life
is suddenly explained by a small carving.

The hurt territories are hurled down
in a storm of beliefs that we always deny.

Whose word was this? Who owns this silence?
I cannot begin until all this ends.

II.

She dances where the numbers end
and we are so moved.

She dances between the farm boys
and the red eyes of old men.

She dances between our dawns
and the old places of night.

She dances where we cannot travel
and gives us the grace to believe.

She dances in a music we cannot
    properly perceive, cannot recreate.

She dances for the past and future
    as we embrace the tired present.

She dances between drums and trumpets
    and the laughter of old lace.

She dances in a separate place
    and we feel the flowing green and gold.

She dances when the music has ceased
    and we have all become inhabited.

She dances to cross those territories that
    only light can truly celebrate.

III.

Who are we when we are not seeking to be
spaced out in a crowd, lost in a zoo, locked
in a dream of becoming and departing?

The old accusations lie around on table tops,
in diaries, in the defective weapons of culture,
between belief and believing.

Travel therefore always appals. Don't get me
wrong; each journey will finally deliver you to
almost the same door.

You leave and we remember your accent but not
the words. We receive letters and forget how you spoke.
We don't hear from you and fidget with the loss.

You stay and we go off. You say it won't be the
same, tell us to follow your route, give us names
and addresses of people who are automatically misplaced.

Does anybody honestly remember you, us, anybody?
Does a single event remain in their minds?
Do you or they actually exist?

PECULIAR OFFERINGS

TELEVISION DREAMS

Whose reality is this? The image of the speaker,
a neutral studio, assurances of truth edited
and timed so that we do not lose other programmes.

There is just so much strength to a story, a given
length of consent; the image reaches out to us
and we rehearse our separate responses

or switch off, over, or let the story filter through
as though its status were enough; the bombing is on;
did we see the news, did we catch it?

The fiction of the thing rings in our lives, we
jump continents and even planets, centuries crunch,
we decipher, totally accept, roll our own.

And so we are fed, fuel injected with data, the busted
ghosts of our culture reinvented, the old
flags on fire or wrapped in semiotics, sweet and neat.

These are not real people. The buildings and vistas we
have seen before. Those voices speak in bubbles;
here is a dead man, saint, a mad cow.

AFTER LONG FASTING

In the terrible white heat of the rain
I was somehow into sea
wave upon wind upon roar of ocean,
the gladiatorial cold, the face a helmet or mask,
the entire body muscle, machine, robed in green flame.

And so I came to this place, to witness,
to be counted, to become one of the number
who hurled prayers, screamed hymns, rang out like
human bells our histories of pain, the world
spinning into tongues of dark belief.

And there, in that communion, did we hear
the God or one of His saints, heaving with laughter
or stitching a riddle into our brains; did He believe
in us for a flash, or did I see into
the terrible mosaic of his howls?

PECULIAR OFFERINGS

I would bring a small stone,
pagan grey, a wind wound at its centre.

I would bring a gorse branch,
the flame dart shaped, stubborn burst of sun.

An arc of bark, lichen laced, odour
of dark sap staining to an ancient sheen.

A thistle, tight flag of fury,
its green exploding into rebellious bouquets.

A poppy head, locket of ancient wounds,
spilling courage onto the fields of constant uncertainty.

PILGRIMS

1

Their sweat bone, their determination
flesh, as the heat of their faith
burns doubt, ridicule, reason.

This fact lights an idea spinning past
the necessary sleep, hunger, the water
and bread made blood.

And in the shallow pits of night
dreams coming like bells or huge birds
to haunt them.

One man saw Christ in a tree
his skull shrieking flame
his wounds like diamonds.

Another ran into tides of ice
so that his body was slashed
into fissures of eternity.

And the youngest, a girl with red hair,
heard the stones speak of futility
as she washed her sores.

2

There is in this gathering a secret song
of shadows and shades and silences
to belong.

There is a declaration beyond the desire
to be here, to be within this community,
to leap out.

To become the energy, the bold
thing itself, yet the slow itch
humility.

The distance between passion and solitude,
the secret carol and the hurled hymn,
the ranging rhododendron and the quiet snowdrop.

Look; here are the words you must obey,
here is the secret of the sign, here is
the centre.

Crawl into this shade, this beginning,
this bud of peace and
embrace the echoes.

3

I cannot do this. My muscles are crazy,
my mind freezes on the sacred text,
I vomit a rainbow.

What I came to do is denied. My vision
is tied in knots. My dream is turned
to grey meat.

The God roars his indifference. He rants
my disbelief. He shakes hail into my
dreams.

I will leave this place tomorrow. I will
cancel all this. I will reconstruct my
truths.

The moon is thistles. A huge rat
rattles within this cell. I can hear
the jester snoring.

When I depart nobody will notice.
My clean shirt will squeak. My tie
will crack the sun.

4

With this faith I robe my life. Between
the trees and the planets God
hurling his certainties.

I enter each day with this prayer. At night
exhaustion enables me to pass through
the dreams that would make me mad.

Joining hands with those who have been here
before, sharing the minds of those who
blaze beside me.

The late night candle becomes the early
light signalling through ancient glass
and onto these stones.

At the centre of the stone total
being, the entire history, the fact
packed into invisibility.

We carry a pebble in one hand and
light in our minds. Sea birds remind us
of the visions of children.

TO CATCH HOLD

Beautiful but not as curiously known,
straight but not so certain, the imperfections recognised.
Trusted but tested also, the acceptance nevertheless slow,
unwilling, capable of rage but a quiet rebellion now.

Arriving at places we have not visited for twenty years, the
churches had become smaller in the mind. Fearing that
everything will have been changed we discover the same light,
the same hills, hedgerows that have changed less than we have.

Returning to Somerset for a funeral in January, I enter
the church hoping to avoid recognition and am swamped
by a fear of faces, the pain of age, the awkwardness of
failing to remember a name, the lichen itch of decay.

It is the voices that are the same. We stand in the
churchyard eager to leap back, to catch hold, to
embrace, as if we were all children, as if each one
of us danced between cascades of rivers and rain.

THE RAIN CHILDREN

Always at a distance, as if this were the greatest trick,
whilst adults crowd to the tragedy or the miracle,
consumed in vast parades, bowed down by rituals;

they escape to the autumn beach, the cold boned
winter park, their voices now tokens driven past evergreens
and the stranded torsos of upturned benches;

and most of all I remember them in the gardens of
large houses, journeying into secret kingdoms, and once
in a Devonshire church a small silent boy

facing me back from a fragment of thirteenth century glass.

OF THESE CATHEDRAL WALLS

Of these cathedral walls and their narrations,
voices as human bells, the clock surrounded by lichen;

a light of grey, gold green, as if ancient in temperature
and depth, an immense weaving of stone so deliberately

made elaborate, poised to praise, to resurrect our faiths,
so that even in ruins there is this grip of God,

the sun and moon adorning, in frost and summer dawns,
the shades of miracles made possible in our minds;

and in one open place, the faces of ten thousand people
gathered to hear a small man's sermons, a pit

becoming a temple, God's roar in their souls, the mind
soaring into psalms, the eloquence of sweat.

THE BLUE

Not always here. Sometimes in other words.
This life entwined within 'the bright rubies of despair'.

Cold, cold in his collection of scowls and screeches,
the invisible shadow-play flashing within his flesh.

Out, out cruel bone; 'let us all be real men'.
The clutched-at carols of success.

And he, now sheltered in whispers, took up his harp
and struck a huge song, became it.

In the corner of the ward we could see it
hurl him from labyrinth to labyrinth,

as if eagles broke from his dreams, as if angels
challenged him with hoops of fire.

And then his going out, his final graces,
a silence so long it lay blue in our hours.

THE GREEN

Old woodlander, the green mind, the presence of it,
observing our coming and going in the east walk cloister.

What time is it for you? Whose praises do you attend?
Does time wait for us here, the green children?

And so the vapour still 'roll down the valleys'
at Wrynose pass, to become 'all the summer long'?

Our toys, our old things, our cherished truths,
seeing ourselves in what we seem to see.

The green of this field; its history deeper
than any word can reach, its sacred horizon.

An idea of the boy Christ coming up from Cornwall,
to trounce the intellect, to light the bone.

IN WINTER STILL

Now the hard land compacts time,
stone winds and the buildings bitten.

Too cold for snow. She waits for ice light
to lift, the creak of sun.

Her husband eats, his sweat reeks of byre,
frozen sacking, damp chains.

He won't speak much, his mind out there still,
wound in a survival game he must win.

Somewhere on the top field blackthorn
prepares its essential trick.

Her kitchen clock lays down the hours.
The radio voice reports from another planet.

THE NIGHT ISLAND

He had seen his father doing this, not doing
a thing recognizable, staring off into the room
as if in another space.

And when, years ahead, is he to see his son
alone on that shore, the spinning planets resting
their existence on the night waters?

ACROSS A WINTER FIELD

Always setting off across a winter field,
the crushed calls of crows and their territories.
Seldom in summer, never with friends; to
people these places with our own perceptions.
Or an animal we hardly describe inhabits
that arena of secret knowledge to kindle
a recognition of ancient realms; a beast
beyond our paradigms rolled into poetry,
the ultimate innocence sensed in history.
The answers to the questions haunt us but
better still the questions themselves. They
keep us solitary, hunched in our own seasons,
visitors between vistas, questing, voyaging.

POET

Between the sun and snow
digging about for words
that will flow
into the history of my soul.

Not to be deceived by nature
or the glitter of dreams
or that fine silence
between our caresses.

Old age may bring back childhood,
the same pathways and trees,
the old games discovered
again and again.

Only set this down, now,
whilst the word sits there,
the honesty and recognition
waiting to begin.

Between the sun and snow
hoping to hear a few
lasting things and celebrate
a real song.

FUTURE

The words are always waiting,
to be used in love or comfort or deceit,
beneath expectations and across worries,
the fidgets and retreats.

Do not trust the very old,
they have gobbled on being for so long
the music and its meaning run together,
the poetry cheats.

Listen mostly to these silences, tap
tap at the open door, and observe where
the places at the table should have been,
and will come.

The mirror is always waiting, the clock has
no memory at all. These words wait
for your eyes and the minds of those
who have not yet heard.

THE ENORMOUS FIELD

The enormous field is where time lies
against a rush of days and other lives.

We stare at trees and hope to sing again
meeting old faces and the truths that outspan pain.

What it is to haunt the future years
and know that single games can surpass fears.

THE MOTH POEM

'Always waiting, moon white moths, leaf cool
collectors of empty rooms, circling where
our words have been....'

He is writing the moth poem. It is November. The
words leak light. Somehow the words lead him
in another direction.

'Always waiting, wheat white moths, the angels
have left them here to observe our doubts,
our circles of desire....'

It is not what he means to say. He sees white sea,
a blue umbrella, a man who writes poems about moths.

'Always waiting, near to window glass, afraid of rain,
suddenly each evening reminding us of age
and the deep heat of numbers
and what we said we would never say....'

The house, hugging the cliff in Cornwall, and
all his childhood days roaring in sea swell,
beach stench, the silence of the telephone.

'Always waiting, never close, missing the present,
hunting of other days when he has tried to write
his poems, his life within the poems....'

The moth, is it aware of his silence? Circling
the lampshade that smells of Cornish autumn,
damp books, raincoats, a man's hat.

'Always waiting, until the words are correct,
too long, too late, the value is damaged;
it does not say what it should....'

The moth, in the corner, observes an ancient scene,
has always been here before, before and before,
always waiting.

UNCERTAIN LIGHT

Is it the light entering
or the departure of a stream of silence
fused through this ancient glass,
this mosaic filter?

Are these hymns, these words pitched
into music, the meaning of truth
or the manner of what we would say
attempting these truths?

And who are we, being here to
declare these things, unable to
settle our doubts and beliefs alone,
collecting such trusts?

Oh we are here to be, to become,
always content to start out,
always happy to leap into
cascades of certainty.

It is only later, alone, huddled
within oneself, that the God or
doubt roars, rattles, fingers the
wound, will not let be.

THE CONVERSATION OF ANGELS

For Rupert Loydell

Not often   these days
   too swift   in   passing
   to judge

or we are always facing
the   other direction
otherwise enthralled

believing it has to be
by holy water   in mountains
the normal world   withering

impossible in crowds
at fairs   in cities
when one wouldn't be able

to recognise a messiah
nailing himself down

or

the conversation of angels

A LIFE

With what words, now, this now, this here,
do I remember, descending, stooping until I stop,
caught between?

With what assent, the mind permitting, the
growl of the soul, the rumour of my life in such
slow motion?

With what ideal ceremony and what intentions and
what plans for the final event, the inevitable
yet unrehearsed farewell?

Ah; do not look at the smile, the simple
shuffle, the dried out jokes, the neat way I have
of reducing sentences.

Do not fool yourself as I become more foolish
than I had planned; my little attempts at redemption
surprise even me.

Standing here in the tap tap of darkness, the
swirl of recognition, the suitcase already packed
with its comforts and deceits.

Shall I meet God the Bone, God the Roar, God
the Monster; and whose hands will reach out in that
terrible music?

With what compassion do I describe this retreat,
this settlement, this pathetic response,
this webbed whisper?

And with what words does this door open, or
close, and what shall I become?